THE GREAT DEPRESSION AND THE NEW DEAL

Heather E. Schwartz

Consultant

Jennifer M. Lopez, NBCT, M.S.Ed.
Teacher Specialist—History/Social Studies
Office of Curriculum & Instruction
Norfolk Public Schools

Publishing Credits

Rachelle Cracchiolo, M.S.Ed., *Publisher*
Conni Medina, M.A.Ed., *Editor in Chief*
Emily R. Smith, M.A.Ed., *Content Director*
Véronique Bos, *Creative Director*
Robin Erickson, *Art Director*
Michelle Jovin, M.A., *Associate Editor*
Mindy Duits, *Senior Graphic Designer*

Image Credits: front cover (left), p.1 Library of Congress [LC-DIG-ppmsca-15614]; front cover (background), p.1, pp.2–3, p.5, p.18 (bottom), pp.20–21, p.27 (top left), p.27 (bottom), p.29 Everett Historical/Shutterstock; p.4 Puttnam/Topical Press Agency/Getty Images; p.6 LOC [LC-DIG-hec-24503]; p.7 (top) Topical Press Agency/Getty Images; p.7 (bottom) LOC [LC-DIG-ppmsca-27871]; p.8 Chronicle/Alamy; p.9 (left), p22 (top) Bettmann Archive/Getty Images; p.9 (right) LOC [LC-USZ62-24155]; p.11, p.13 (right) U.S. National Archives; pp.12–13 New York Public Library; pp.14–15 LOC [LC-USF34-014751]; p.17 (top right) LOC [LC-DIG-ppmsca-03054]; p.18 (top left) LOC [LC-J601-302]; p.18 (center) LOC [LC-USZ62-105105]; p.19 Forest Service Northern Region; p.20 (left) LOC [LC-USW33-015690-ZC]; p.21 (top right) LOC [LC-USZC2-1265]; p.22 (bottom) Courtesy Everett Collection/ Newscom; p.23 LOC [LC-USZ62-27663]; p.24 (bottom) LOC [LC-DIG-fsac-1a35371]; pp.24–25 LOC [LC-DIG-fsac-1a35442]; p.25 (right) FDR Presidential Library & Museum; p.26 LOC [LC-DIG-ds-04632]; p.28 (left) LOC [LC-DIG-fsac-1a34169]; p.28 (right) LOC [LC-USF34-018227-C]; p.32 LOC [LC-DIG-fsa-8b29516]; all other images from iStock and/or Shutterstock.

TCM Teacher Created Materials
5301 Oceanus Drive
Huntington Beach, CA 92649-1030
www.tcmpub.com
ISBN 978-1-4258-5068-5

Printed in China WAI002

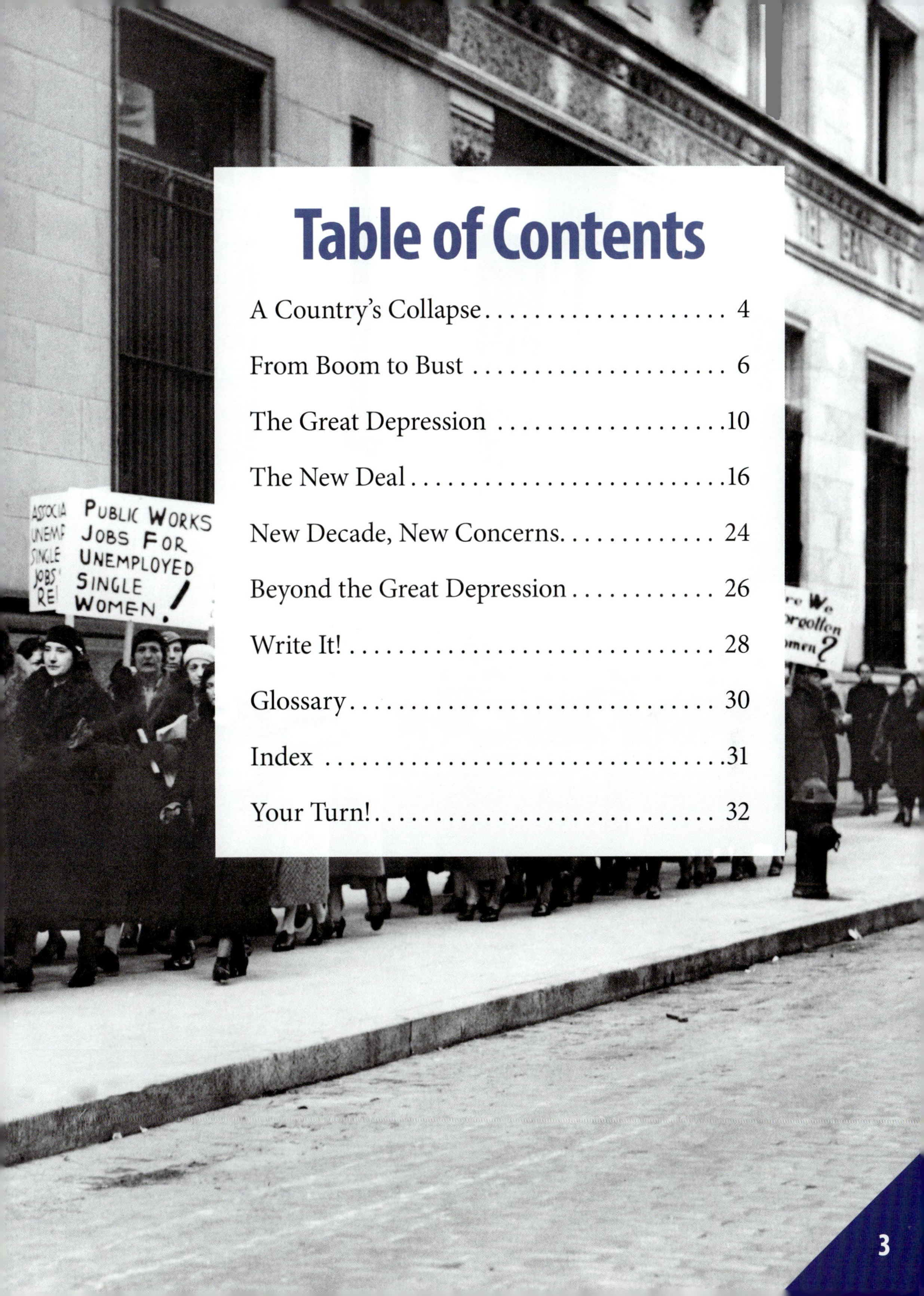

Table of Contents

A Country's Collapse

The beginning of the twentieth century was a time of change for the United States. During the 1920s, many people lived lives of luxury. As the U.S. economy moved more toward an **industrialized** society, some people struggled. But for many, life was easy. They had good jobs and money to spend. They overlooked—and sometimes even ignored—the signs that trouble was brewing. The U.S. economy was about to collapse.

In 1929, the worst happened, and millions of people lost their jobs. People were homeless and hungry. In the first few years of the Great Depression, people could not get the help they needed from the government. They were frustrated, scared, and angry. More than anything, they were ready for change.

▼ A carload of people celebrate in early 1929.

Franklin Delano Roosevelt (also known as FDR) was elected president in 1932. He promised to help people. He said he had a plan to fix the economy. This plan was called the New Deal, and it addressed the problems of the Great Depression. It also put programs in place that would help people find work while helping the country as a whole. This plan changed the way people felt about their country and their government. Life in the United States would never be the same.

President Hoover

Before FDR, Herbert Hoover was president. Hoover had served as the head of the Food Administration during World War I. His job was to keep people fed. He gave food to people at home, as well as to millions of starving Europeans. Hoover became president in 1928. In a speech, he said the United States was closer to ending **poverty** "than ever before in the history of any land." One year later, the Great Depression began.

▼ An unemployed man stands near his home in 1933.

Recycling at Its Roots

During the Great Depression, people learned to be resourceful. If they couldn't afford coal, then they burned corn to heat their homes. They sewed their own clothing and saved items to be reused in other ways.

From Boom to Bust

Before the Great Depression, the U.S. economy was doing well. The United States was becoming a society of **consumers**. Then, Americans saw their world come crashing down.

The Roaring Twenties

In the 1920s, business was booming in the United States. Many people had jobs and money to spend. People bought cars, radios, and telephones for the first time. Not everyone could afford to buy those things using cash. Instead, they bought goods using **credit**.

Society was changing too. American troops had returned home from World War I. They wanted to celebrate their victory overseas. People started shopping in chain stores, such as JCPenney, Macy's, and Sears. Many Americans listened to the same music as each other. They spoke alike and used the same slang words. People drove similar cars. All these things created a society based on a **mass culture**.

The Stock Market

The stock market is a list of companies that are selling stocks, or parts of ownership in their companies. When the companies make money, people who own stocks in those companies make money too. They share the **profits**. The most important stock exchange is the New York Stock Exchange, located in Manhattan. It was founded in 1817.

Age of the Automobile

By 1929, there was one car on the road for every five Americans. Ford's Model T® was the most popular car. Its low cost meant a lot of people could afford it. When people began buying on credit, companies made cars that were more comfortable, stylish, and expensive.

◀ 1921 Model T in front of the White House

Americans looked toward the future. When people **invested** in the stock market, they expected the good times to go on and on. They thought the companies they invested in would keep growing and making money.

The flapper style of dress was popular in the 1920s.

This 1912 cartoon shows people gathered around a ticker tape machine, reading stock prices.

The Crash

The good times eventually came to an end. Economic growth slowed, **unemployment rates** rose, and stock prices dropped. People began to panic. They could only make money if they sold their stocks at higher prices than what they had paid for them. If stock prices fell, they would lose money.

On Thursday, October 24, 1929, panic turned into action as large numbers of people started selling their stocks as fast as they could. Everyone hoped to sell before prices dropped even more. However, as the panic continued into the following week, the mass selling made the problem worse. No one wanted to buy, and with no **demand**, prices fell even more rapidly.

BROOKLYN DAILY EAGLE

And Complete Long Island News

LATE NEWS

WALL STREET 1:15 PRICES ★★

★ NEW YORK CITY, THURSDAY, OCTOBER 24, 1929. ★

32 PAGES

THREE CENTS

89th YEAR—No. 295.

WALL ST. IN PANIC AS STOCKS CRASH

Attempt Made to Kill Italy's Crown Prince

STOCKS CRASH IN RUSH TO SELL; BILLIONS LOST

Morgan, Mitchell Buying Stocks in Effort to Check Rush to Unload.

ASSASSIN CAUGHT IN BRUSSELS MOB; PRINCE UNHURT

Royal Suitor Was About to Lay Wreath on Unknown Soldiers' Tomb.

Princess, Deeply Moved, Falls Into Fiance's Arms and Kisses Him

ATTEMPT MADE ON LIFE

Crown Prince Humbert.

Hollywood Fire Destroys Films Worth Millions

Consolidated Studios Are Swept by Flames Fatal to One—Master Pictures Burned Include Many New Talkie Productions.

FEAR 52 PERISHED IN LAKE MICHIGAN; FERRY IS MISSING

Wreckage Picked Up Indicates Craft Went Down With All Aboard.

PIECE OF PLANE LIKE DITEMAN'S IS FOUND AT SEA

Black and Orange Wreckage Indicates Daring Flier Went to Death.

High Duty Group Gave $700,000 to Coolidge Drive

Grundy Agrees Rates Went Up Due to His Activities as Propagandist, Favors More Lobbying to 'Carry Out Voters' Wish.'

FOR MORE LOBBYISTS

JOSEPH R. GRUNDY

CARNEGIE CHARGE OF PAID ATHLETES ROUSES COLLEGES

HOOVER'S TRAIN HALTED BY AUTO PLACED ON RAILS

WARDER SOUGHT TO KEEP SEA TRIP SECRET, AID SAYS

SOMERS NAMED AS HEAD OF NEW EXCHANGE BANK

Survey Finds Shopping for Stars Is General. Remedies Now in Force.

2 Negroes Admit Scheme to Collect Insurance for Loss of Machine

Woman Testifies She Was Asked to Say Nothing About Plans.

Damman Is Chosen for Chairman of Board, Miller Vice President.

newspaper front page from October 24, 1929

On Tuesday, October 29, the stock market crashed. This day was later called Black Tuesday. People had spent a lot of their money buying stocks. Those same stocks were now worthless. Many people owed money. They had bought stocks on credit to begin with. They had to pay back the borrowed money.

People with money in the stock market were not the only ones affected by the crash. Companies with stocks lost everything too. Jobs across the country were now at risk. Owners had to dismiss employees or close their businesses.

▲ This man paid around $1,500 for this car and is trying to sell it for $100.

Unhappy Holidays

Les Orear was in college when the stock market crashed. He had to move back to Chicago to help support his family. Orear found a job that paid 37.5 cents a day. He has no memories of Thanksgiving or Christmas during this time. He said these two days weren't celebrated as holidays—they were just days without pay.

Misguided Guidance

President Hoover urged Americans not to panic. He wanted them to rely on what he called "rugged individualism." He thought the crisis would soon pass. He said Americans could get through the hard times without the government's help.

The Great Depression

Global Impact

In 1930, President Hoover signed the Tariff Act. This law raised taxes on goods from other countries by 20 percent. It was meant to encourage people to buy things from the United States. Hoover thought it would help U.S. companies. However, the new law spread the United States' economic problems around the world. After that, global trade suffered.

Coin Crisis

Before the Great Depression, the government issued $2.50, $5, $10, and $20 gold coins. These gold coins were called *eagles*. Eagles were made of their weight in gold. During the depression, the government stopped making gold coins. To this day, the government has never made gold coins for everyday use again.

As the stock market plunged, people began to worry about their money in banks. What if the same thing that happened to the stock market happened to their savings? Would their money still be there in the future? Once again, mass concern led to mass action. Many people rushed to withdraw their money at the same time. This is called a *bank run*.

The problem with bank runs is that banks do not store everyone's cash in the bank. Banks use some of the money to grant loans, which they can charge **interest** on. Banks also invest some of the money, which helps them to earn profits. Banks only keep enough cash on hand to meet a reasonable demand for cash on any given day.

When large numbers of people tried to empty their accounts in late 1929, bank managers gave out all the cash they had. Then, bank managers sold goods and properties at whatever low prices they were offered. Panic and bank runs actually created the problem many people feared. By 1933, one out of every five banks in the United States had gone **bankrupt**. People who did not withdraw their money in time lost it forever.

1929 bank run

Hungry and Homeless

As the Great Depression continued, the American way of life completely changed. People took whatever work they could find. In New York City, close to six thousand people sold apples for five cents each. Some of those workers included former millionaires.

Unemployment and low wages meant people could not afford basic goods. Packed **tenements** grew even more crowded as families moved in together. People could not afford much food to eat or coal for heat. Some people found relief in cities. The government did not offer much help. But soup kitchens and breadlines gave out free food.

When people could not afford their rent and house payments, they were forced to live on the streets. Many people became homeless. They lived in *shantytowns*, which were crude towns packed with homemade dwellings. Some houses were made out of cardboard or tin. Others were tents or even holes dug into the dirt.

▼ This shantytown was built near New York City in 1933.

Hating Hoover

Charles Michelson was a leader in the Democratic Party. He was the first person to use the term *Hoovervilles* to describe shantytowns. People blamed President Hoover for failing to help them. So, Hoover's name was used in insulting ways. People named the newspapers they slept under "Hoover blankets." The cardboard they used to replace shoe soles was called "Hoover leather."

Soup Kitchens

The idea of soup kitchens came from Irish **immigrants**. During the Great Hunger in Ireland, people served free meals to those who were hungry. During the Great Depression, Americans did the same. An unexpected owner ran one of the best soup kitchens at this time. Famed criminal Al Capone fed thousands of people from his soup kitchen (shown above) every day.

Dust Bowl

People struggled to find jobs in cities during the Great Depression. However, life was not any better for people living in rural areas. In particular, people in the Great Plains region struggled. Their problems had begun years earlier, during World War I. During the war, demand for wheat was high, and farmers could make money. They destroyed their fields as they grew more and more wheat.

Dust Bowl Size

The Dust Bowl spanned parts of Oklahoma, Texas, Kansas, Colorado, and New Mexico. In total, it was 300,000 square miles (777,000 square kilometers). That is larger than all of Germany. Dirt from the Dust Bowl traveled as far as Illinois. It also darkened skies all along the East Coast of the United States.

No Bonus for Vets

In 1932, more than 12,000 homeless **veterans** marched on Washington, DC. They wanted early payments of bonuses they were owed. They called themselves the Bonus Army. Congress would not pass a bill to help the veterans. President Hoover sent in troops to stop the protest. Violence broke out. One veteran was shot and killed. Several people were injured. This event was a huge embarrassment for President Hoover.

a dust storm in Kansas ▼

Then, in 1931, it didn't rain much, and there were lots of high winds in the Great Plains. The high winds blew the dry **topsoil**, which resulted in thick dust storms. Because of these storms, this area became known as the Dust Bowl. The dust storms were so dense that they were often called "black blizzards." During bad dust storms, there was **zero visibility**. People got infections and died from inhaling too much dust.

Crop failures also led to food shortages for **livestock**. This combination forced many farmers into poverty. Families pulled together and helped their neighbors when they could. They created community programs to lift their spirits. Still, survival was difficult. Many farmers lost their land to banks. When they could not make the payments they owed, banks took the land back.

Hundreds of thousands of people left the Great Plains during the Great Depression. Some people snuck on trains. Other people filled their cars with everything they could fit and drove away. They were searching for work and better lives. No matter where they went, they struggled to find either.

The New Deal

Many people blamed President Hoover for their problems during the Great Depression. A new president brought fresh ideas to rescue the country.

FDR Takes Office

In 1932, Franklin Delano Roosevelt ran for president. He promised the country a fresh start if elected. Later that year, he won in a landslide victory. When FDR took office, the country was in its worst year of the Great Depression. One in four American adults could not find a job. Most of the banks throughout the country had failed.

1933

- Mar. 4: FDR is sworn in as president and begins his New Deal plan.
- Mar. 6: FDR closes all banks as part of his "bank holiday" plan.
- Mar. 9–June 16: FDR's "Hundred Days" programs begin, with 13 major laws passed in 14 weeks.

1934

- May 10: One of the worst dust storms of the Dust Bowl period hits, convincing people to move out of the Dust Bowl region.
- Nov. 6: Democratic Party wins Senate seats in the midterm elections, which serves as a show of support for FDR's policies.

1935

- May 27: The Supreme Court rules that one of FDR's acts is **unconstitutional**.
- Aug. 14: FDR signs the Social Security Act, which still exists.
- Aug. 31: FDR states that the United States will not involve itself in international wars.

FDR took swift action. His plan for the country became known as the New Deal, and it was based on "the three Rs." *Relief* would stop the economy from getting worse. *Recovery* would start to turn things around. *Reform* would focus on changing laws to stop this from happening again.

Saving the banking industry was FDR's first priority. He closed American banks for four days, which gave Congress time to pass the Emergency Banking Act. Under the new law, banks could not reopen until they passed an inspection. They had to prove they would not fail.

1936

- Jan. 6: The Supreme Court rules another of FDR's acts is unconstitutional.
- Jan. 24: Against FDR's requests, Congress approves the payment of bonuses to veterans.
- Nov. 3: FDR wins a second term as president.

1937

- Feb. 2: FDR introduces a bill to reorganize the judiciary system, but loses many of his long-term supporters.
- May: FDR cuts government spending, leading to a rise in unemployment rates for the first time since he took office.

1938

- Jan. 3: FDR recommends building up the armed services.
- June: Unemployment rates go down.
- Sep. 27: FDR asks for a peaceful end to Germany's aggression.

Portraits with Purpose

Dorothea Lange took photos of American farmers during the Great Depression. She took notes on what they said and what she saw. A government agency used her pictures. They wanted Americans to see the harsh conditions people in rural places were facing. Lange's photos are still some of the most famous images from this time.

"Brother, Can You Spare a Dime?"

In 1932, musician E. Y. Harburg released a new song called "Brother, Can You Spare a Dime?" The song spoke to many Americans during the Great Depression. The lyrics told the story of a man who had worked hard for his country but still wound up in poverty and standing in breadlines.

Carver's Cure

As the CCC restored damaged soil, George Washington Carver (shown above) was working to solve for the future. Carver was a scientist and a genius with plants. He encouraged farmers to plant vegetables and legumes in their new fields. These crops add nitrogen to soil, which keeps soil healthy. Carver also introduced crop rotation to the South. With this process, farmers plant different crops in fields in back-to-back years. It allows the soil time to recover. Crop rotation is still used.

CCC Accomplishments

The CCC ended in 1942. Over three million people worked for the agency. The workers repaired millions of acres of soil. They also planted more than two billion trees.

Government Relief

FDR formed new government agencies as part of his New Deal. Americans knew many of these agencies by the first letters in their names. They were called the *alphabet agencies*.

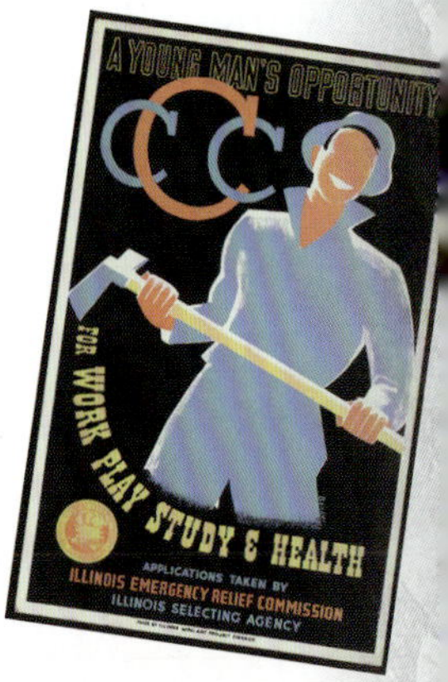

One of the most popular agencies was the Civilian Conservation Corps (CCC). It was formed in April 1933. The goal of the CCC was to fight unemployment and repair soil for farmers. The CCC offered jobs to young men. They worked on projects in the Great Plains and on federal land, including national forests and parks. They lived in camps and worked for six months at a time.

Many alphabet agencies, such as the CCC, were temporary. They were meant to provide relief during a time of crisis. Other agencies were permanent. Congress formed the Federal Deposit Insurance Corporation (FDIC) two months after the CCC. The FDIC backed people's money when it was held in banks. The FDIC is still around. It guarantees that people will not lose all their money if banks fail.

▼ A tourist at the Nez Perce National Forest drives on a road that was built by the CCC.

Saving the Country

The New Deal continued to improve the country throughout FDR's first term. He founded more agencies. A lot of them gave jobs to people who were out of work. The Civil Works Administration (CWA) gave jobs to **laborers**. They improved bridges, hospitals, schools, parks, playgrounds, and airports. Students and young people found jobs with the National Youth Administration (NYA). Parts of the Works Progress Administration (WPA) offered jobs to artists. The WPA employed 8.5 million people. Some of them wrote, drew, or painted what they saw. Other people took photographs or wrote music.

FDR's new agencies did more than create jobs. They helped stop future disasters too. The Tennessee Valley Authority (TVA) controlled floods and added electrical power to the Tennessee River area. The Securities and Exchange Commission (SEC) kept watch over the stock market. It worked to prevent another crash.

By 1935, things were looking better. FDR ran for re-election. The country was starting to come out of the Great Depression. Many people gave credit to FDR. So, FDR won a second term.

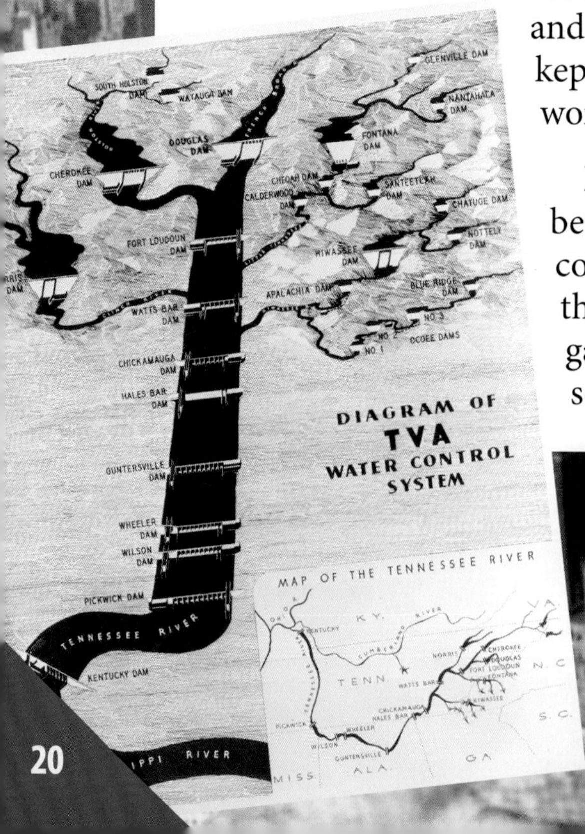

This diagram shows the planned work for the TVA.

▼ A laborer helps build the Empire State Building in 1930.

Art Appreciation

The WPA built roads, bridges, parks, and airports. It also supported artists and writers. Some people felt using money to support art was a waste. But the director of the WPA thought artists deserved to be paid for their work too. The WPA backed the making of 2,566 murals and 17,744 sculptures.

You're Hired!

Some famous structures were built during the depression. The Empire State Building was finished in 1931 and provided over three thousand jobs each day. Two years later, construction began on the Golden Gate Bridge. Hundreds of men came from around the country to work on the huge structure. The pay ranged from $4 to $11 per day, which was a lot of money at the time!

A Changing Culture

As the 1930s stretched on, the economy slowly improved. At the same time, the culture of the United States was changing. Music, novels, and sports were inspiring Americans.

One of the most famous musicians of this time was Duke Ellington. Ellington wrote swing music and led a band in live performances. *Swing* is a type of jazz that is upbeat. When people heard swing music, they became hopeful for a better future. When Ellington performed, large crowds gathered to lift their spirits.

▲ Mitchell holding her novel

Owen's Attempts

Despite Hitler's racist views, many German people loved Owens. During the long-jump competition, Owens did a practice run. When he learned his practice run counted as one of his attempts, he was flustered. That embarrassment caused Owens to mess up his second attempt. With only one chance left to make it to the finals, a German athlete named Carl Long approached Owens. Long gave Owens advice and calmed him down. Long's suggestions helped Owens make it to the finals on his third attempt. In the finals, Owens beat Long for the gold medal.

Scarlett's Success

Gone With the Wind won the Pulitzer Prize. That is an award for the best writing each year. It became one of the most widely read books of the twentieth century. It has sold 30 million copies and has been translated into more than 40 languages.

While some people wanted to feel better, other people wanted to have their pain understood. Margaret Mitchell did just that. In 1936, Mitchell released *Gone With the Wind.* The novel follows Scarlett O'Hara. Though her life is hard, O'Hara refuses to give up. Readers related to O'Hara. They saw themselves in her. If she didn't give up, neither would they.

In the same year readers were falling in love with *Gone With the Wind*, sports fans had their own hero. Jesse Owens was a track-and-field star. He competed in the 1936 Olympic Games® in Berlin. Germany's leader—Adolf Hitler—discriminated against people of different **races**. Owens—a black athlete—won four gold medals, sending a powerful message to Hitler. Owens also set a world record that stood for 25 years.

The country was recovering. It was also changing.

Owens at the 1936 Olympic Games ▶

New Decade, New Concerns

The economy continued to recover. FDR felt it was time to pull back spending on government programs. However, it was too soon. Companies failed and people lost their jobs again. A **recession** took over the country in 1937. This period was nicknamed "Roosevelt's Recession." FDR quickly returned to government spending. Once again, the economy steadied.

By the end of 1938, the New Deal was losing support. It had solved many problems, but the country was faced with new issues. British and French leaders had declared war on Germany. The Soviet Union, Japan, and many other countries were also involved. In 1939, the New Deal ended as the nation's leaders shifted their focus. Two years later, the United States entered World War II.

▼ In 1943, a worker assembles a plane to be used in the war.

It was a scary time for Americans, but the war helped the U.S. economy. Unemployed people could now find jobs. More than 16 million men and women joined the military. Even more people found jobs helping the war effort from home. They made weapons and other goods needed for the war.

Many Americans still struggled. However, their outlook grew more positive. People wanted to help win the war and work for world peace. With the U.S. entry into World War II, the Great Depression officially came to an end.

There's a Limit

FDR did not think that the country should switch presidents at the start of a major war. He announced that he was running for president again. FDR was elected to a third term in 1940. He was re-elected for a fourth term in 1944. In 1947, Congress passed the Twenty-Second Amendment. It limits U.S. presidents to two terms.

After the War

In 1945, FDR died. It was only months before the end of the war. His **approval rating** at the time was 70 percent. This is the highest approval rating of any president on record. With so many people spending money after the war, the economy grew without him.

Beyond the Great Depression

Changing Views

One of the biggest impacts of the New Deal was the effect it had on people's opinions. Before the Great Depression, Americans felt that the government should stay out of people's lives. After the New Deal, many people changed their views. They felt it was the duty of the government to support its people. They also thought the government should make sure its economy was strong.

New Deal Lives On

Several programs grew from New Deal programs. The WPA led to the development of other national programs to fund the arts. The CCC serves as a model for the 21st Century Conservation Service Corps. The welfare program still exists. So does the Social Security program.

By the time the Great Depression ended, the unemployment rate had dropped to its lowest point in decades. At the height of the depression, 1 in 4 Americans was unemployed. When FDR died, it was about 1 in 50 people. People who lived through this time would never forget it. For many people, to survive meant to struggle. Americans were already hard workers. Now, they became resourceful too. They learned to use what money and materials they had wisely. They tried not to waste things, and they saved for the future.

FDR's New Deal programs and policies bettered the lives of millions of people. They improved the country's landscape. They also left a legacy for the future. New Deal programs were designed to protect against another crisis. The effects of the Great Depression led to lasting change. Even programs that ended decades ago have helped shape modern life in the United States.

By the end of the Great Depression, Americans had proven their strength when times were tough. Their experiences became a part of history. The lessons learned were passed on to future generations.

▲ The New Deal's Home Owners' Loan Corporation agency kept over a million people from becoming homeless.

This poster advertises the Social Security program, a New Deal program that still exists. ▶

Write It!

Imagine you are living during the Great Depression. How has your life changed since the 1920s? Has anyone in your family left home to look for work? How do you try to help out with chores and earning money? What do you do for fun? Consider whether you live in the city or country. You can look back through the book for details about urban and rural experiences.

Write some ideas about your imaginary life. Then, write a letter to a friend about your everyday struggles during the Great Depression.

Glossary

approval rating—a percentage of people who think someone is doing a good job

bankrupt—unable to pay debts

consumers—people who buy and use goods

credit—money given to purchase goods that a person later repays

demand—a desire and ability to buy goods or services at a certain time and price

immigrants—people who come to countries to live there

industrialized—describes a society with highly developed industries

interest—a charge for borrowed money

invested—used money to buy stock, property, or other things in order to make more money

laborers—people who do physical work for pay

livestock—farm animals that are kept for profit and use

mass culture—a set of similar values and ideas that form out of a common exposure to the same music, media, news, and art

poverty—the state of being without money or possessions

profits—money that is made after all expenses have been taken out

races—groups of people with common ancestries

recession—a period of time in which there is a decrease in economic activity and many people do not have jobs

tenements—apartment buildings that house especially poorer families in cities

topsoil—surface soil that a farmer turns over when plowing

unconstitutional—not agreeing with or according to the constitution of a society or country

unemployment rates—the total number of people in places who are looking for jobs but have not been hired yet

veterans—former members of the armed forces

zero visibility—the state of being unable to see anything due to poor weather, darkness, fog, or smoke

Index

Your Turn!

This photograph is known as "Migrant Mother." The photographer was Dorothea Lange. Lange was hired by the government as part of the Farm Security Administration Program. Lange's job was to bring awareness to farmers who were suffering and convince people that they needed help. Lange took this photograph in 1936 in Nipomo, California. The mother pictured is Florence Owens Thompson. Thompson is believed to have left the Dust Bowl with her seven children so she could find work in California. This photograph was published in many magazines and newspapers of the time. Thompson became a symbol for the harsh realities that farm workers were facing during the Great Depression.

Imagine you are the editor of a newspaper or magazine. You have just been sent Lange's photograph. You know that Thompson and many other people are suffering. Design the layout of your newspaper or magazine. Include an article about the "Migrant Mother" photograph.